Hey, kids!
See if you can spot Santa,
Mrs. Claus and Reindeer
hidden throughout
the story.

To....colette...

You made it onto Santa's NICE list – WELL DONE!

MERRY CHRISTMAS!

Love from.........

I SAW SANTA IN AUSTRALIA

Written by J.D. Green

Illustrated by Nadja Sarell and Srimalie Bassani

LAKE PRESS

anta's not planned his holiday this year.
Mrs. Claus says, 'Shall we go to Australia, my dear?
You've told us how it is your favourite place,
but remember, the children should not see your face.'

'Yes, Australia!' says Santa. 'That place has it all!
Great sights, tasty bites, super shops, big and small.'

Mrs. Claus says, 'Let's pack. We can head off tonight!
Remember what I said? You must keep out of sight!'

The sleigh's loaded up. They are keen to explore.
There is so much to see on their big Australian tour.
Through Perth and Adelaide and Melbourne they go.
'I love being back!' Santa says. 'Ho! Ho! Ho!'

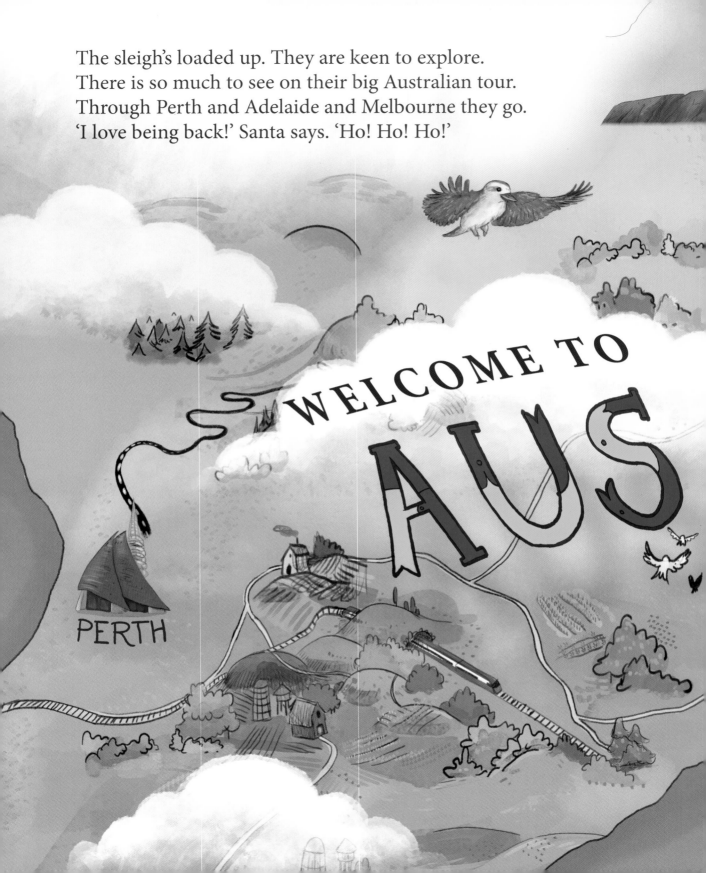

WELCOME TO
AUS

PERTH

TRALIA

ADELAIDE

MELBOURNE

It's a family tradition, when they go away,
to buy a few gifts to remember their stay.

So smart Mrs. Claus came prepared with a list,
she knows what to buy, and no friend will be missed.

Santa thinks buying nice gifts is quite tough.
He's feeling confused – there's just so much stuff!

His basket soon fills up with goodies galore,
such as meat pies, lamingtons, pavlova and more.

Reindeer is dressed in a clever disguise,
so he will not be spotted by keen little eyes.

He's ready to sight-see and have lots of fun,
visiting each cool new place, one by one.

The Clauses are done buying gifts for their friends,
it's time for sight-seeing before their trip ends.

But at the North Pole, Head Elf checks the mail.
He opens one letter and turns very pale…

Dear Santa,

I want to be an astronaut when I grow up.
I would love a silver space suit for Christmas.

Please.

Love, Noah xxx
Age 5
from Bankstown

P.S. Did I see you at the Australia Museum?
There was a guy with a big, white beard
playing inside a rocket and eating
freeze-dried ice cream! Was it you?

Dear Santa,

My favourite place in the whole wide world is the ocean! Please can I have a snorkel and flippers for Christmas? Thank you!

By the way, I was at Wet'n'Wild yesterday. I didn't have my glasses on while I was swimming, but I saw someone with a big, white beard and a red-and-white bathing suit. Was it you? Please write back and tell me.

Love, Emma
Age 7
from Broadbeach Waters

At home in the North, Head Elf says, 'This won't do!
One sighting is terrible – now we've had two!'

Santa really should be taking more care,
it seems more children have spotted him there.

Dear Santa,

I would love, love, love a big, pink unicorn!
I drew one for you here.

Love, Bella x X x
Age 5¾
from Nowra

P.S. Did I see you at the Blue Mountains
National Park, wearing green hiking boots
and a red-and-white striped backpack?
It even sounded like you were whistling,
'Waltzing Matilda.'

Am I right?

BLUE
MOUNTAINS
NATIONAL
PARK

Reading the mail, Head Elf shakes his head.
This letter has caused him to turn slightly red!

Hey, Santa!

Was that you at Parliament House? I was
there with my best friend, Bobby. I know you
live in the North Pole, but it really looked just
like you sitting on a bench, wearing sunglasses
and drinking a milkshake. Oh, and we would
like new cricket bats for Christmas, please!

Bye!
William
Age 7
from Canberra

In the North Pole, Head Elf can't believe what he's seeing, another *two* children have seen Santa fleeing!

Hello Santa,

My name is Olivia and I am 6½.
I love horseback riding and would like new boots for Christmas.

I went to the Perth Royal Show. Did you go, too? I'm pretty sure I saw you riding a horse while eating a hot dog!

Was that really you?

Love, Olivia
from Scarborough

HOT

ALBERT
PARK
LAKE

NO SLEIGHS
ALLOWED

Hi Santa,

I am 8 and I would like a real duck for Christmas. My grandpa and I were watching the ducks at Albert Park Lake when we saw a big, red sleigh on the other side of the pond. I heard the park ranger say sleighs do not float.

Was that you?

James
from South Yarra

The holiday's over; the shopping is done.
Australia was brilliant – they had so much fun!

Now they are home, Head Elf lets Santa know,
he's been spotted by children in Australia. Oh, no!

Noah, age 5

Dear Noah,

Yes, you did spot me at the museum! I was on my summer holiday in Australia. Enjoy your silver space suit.

Love, Santa x

Emma, age 7

Dear Emma,

Yes, you did spot me at the water park! Australia is my favourite place to visit. Have fun with your snorkel and flippers.

Love, Santa x

Bella, age 5¾

Dear Bella,

Yes, you did spot me at the National Park! I was on my summer holiday in Australia. Have fun with your pink unicorn!

Love, Santa x

Mrs. Claus says to Santa, 'I know what to do.
We can make this all good with a letter or two.'

Olivia, age 6½

William, age 7

James, age 8

When Christmas arrives, all the children who wrote
get one extra gift, and inside is a note…

Hello little one,

On my summer break, I like getting away,
so I go to Australia, the best place to stay.
There's so much in Australia I like to see,
there's really no place that I'd rather be.

So keep a lookout, `cause you never know,
if I might be somewhere that you like to go.
And if you can find time I like nothing better,
than hearing from you, so write me a letter!
Merry Christmas!
Love,

Santa

xxx

LAKE PRESS

Lake Press Pty Ltd
5 Burwood Road
Hawthorn VIC 3122 Australia
Email: publishing@lakepress.com.au
www.lakepress.com.au

Written by J.D. Green
Illustrated by Nadja Sarell and Srimalie Bassani
Designed by Geff Newland

First published 2018
Printed in China 5 4 3 2 1
LP18 764

Hey, kids! Flick back and see if you can spot Santa, Mrs. Claus and Reindeer hidden throughout the story.